Mark McCraw

It Happens!

Illustrated by Iris Davydenko

Copyright © 2024   **Mark H. McCraw**

All rights reserved. No part of this book may be reproduced in any form or by any electronic or mechanical means, including information storage and retrieval systems, without permission in writing from the author, except by reviewers, who may quote brief passages in a review.

ISBN: **979-8-218-40927-2**

Permission to use material:

Illustrator: **Iris Davydenko**
Editor: **Tram Bui**
Credits for the cover design: **Iris Davydenko**
Printed in the United States of America.

For more information or requests, please contact the author, Mark McCraw, at markmccraw@ markmccraw.com.
Reviews can be made online: amazon.com, walmart.com, barnesandnoble.com, and booksamillion.com.

This is a work of fiction.
Any names, characters, businesses, locations, events, or incidents are fictitious.
Any resemblance to actual persons, living or dead, places, or actual events is purely coincidental.

This book is dedicated to accident-prone people.

My name is Allen, the Accident-Prone Kid.
I am a first grader. I often have accidents in
public, at school, and at home.

It is tough being an accident-prone kid.

When I have accidents,
I tell adults:

"It is okay!
It happens!"

This is the story
of my accident-prone life.

When I brought my plate from the kitchen,
I spilled it.
Daddy was upset with me. I said,

"It is okay!
It happens!"

When I spilled my milk at school in the
cafeteria,
the cafeteria worker said,

"It is okay!
It happens!"

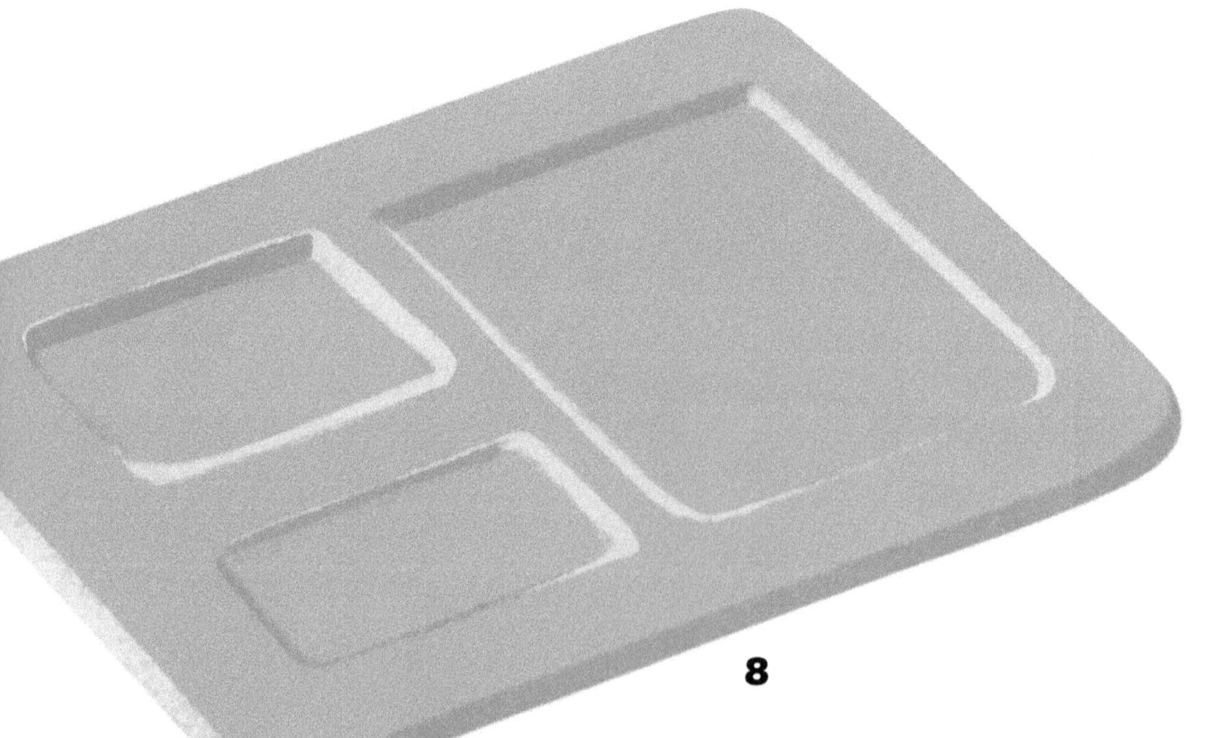

When I stubbed my toe on the couch and
cried to Mommy,
she said,

"It is okay!
It happens!"

When my Aunt Charlene saw me drop my
ice cream cone on the road,
my aunt said:

"I will get you another one
at the ice cream shop".

She told me,
"It is okay!
It happens!"

Daddy and Mommy told me,

"If you break something
in a store, you must pay for it."

My parents told me this so I could be careful
around glass and other items.
However, I broke a bottle.

Instead, the grocery store worker told me,

"It is okay!
It happens!"

Fresh Milk
MILK
Milk

When I went to school, my teacher asked me
to turn my homework in.
She asked,

"What is your excuse for not handing it in?"

I told her that my dog ate my homework
which he did.
My teacher said,

"It is okay!
It happens!"

One time, I was embarrassed at school. I had
been playing hard at recess and forgot to go
to the bathroom, so I had a bad bathroom
accident. My teacher said,
"I will call your mom and check your
backpack for other clothes."

She told me,
"It is okay!
It happens!"

When I broke the watch Daddy had given me,
he said,

"It is okay!
It happens!"

When I fell in the mud while playing at
recess,
my teacher told me,

"It is okay!
It happens!"

I learned that accidents happen, whether you
are an adult, or a child like me.

"It is okay!
It happens!"

ABOUT THE AUTHOR

I am a former elementary school teacher, Air Force and Air Force Reserve military member, adjunct professor, daycare teacher, migrant Head Start teacher, corrections officer, pastor, and non-profit executive. I am also the Oklahoma Commissioner for the Scottish MacRae family, Korea Defense Veterans Association (K.D.V.A.) member, American Legion Member and Boy's State Recruiter in Oklahoma for my post, and Disabled American Veterans (D.A.V.) member and officer serving two terms as a second junior vice commander.

Currently, I am a member of the Society of Children's Book Writers and Illustrators (S.C.B.W.I.), the Oklahoma Literacy Association (O.L.A.), the Oklahoma Writers Federation Inc. (O.W.F.I.), and American Library Association (A.L.A.).

I have an associate degree in criminal justice, a bachelor's degree in theology, a master's degree in elementary education, a master's degree in curriculum and instruction, and two years of doctoral courses. This is my tenth published book, with many more to come!

CHILDREN'S BOOK AUTHOR/
AIR FORCE VETERAN
Mark McCraw
Children's Book Author
Don't Do Without. Scout it Out!
www.markmccraw.com
www.markmccraw.com

<u>**MAJOR RETAILERS AND OTHER WEBSITES:**</u>

Mark McCraw's books are available online at Barnes and Noble, Target, Books-A-Million, Bookshop, and the official Mark McCraw website.

Please check out Mark McCraw and other veteran authors at https://patriotwrites.com/. You can also listen to Mark McCraw on Author's Alcove: Writers Helping Writers on Spotify.

OTHER WEBSITES:

Mark McCraw's books are available in over twenty different countries and global sites. Visit his website at www.markmccraw.com for more purchase options.

<u>**AUDIBLES, KINDLES, HARDCOVER, AND SOFTCOVER**</u>

Some books are also available on Audible, Kindle, and in hardcover. Visit www.amazon.com for more details.

E-BOOKS

Rakuten Kobo
Apple Books
Everand
Tolino
Overdrive
Bibliotheca
Baker and Taylor
Odilo
Vivlio
Borrow Box
Smashwords
Gardners
Palace Marketplace
Barnes and Noble

LOCAL LIBRARIES:

Oklahoma Library

Metropolitan Library System

Florida Libraries

Santa Rosa County Library-Five books
Okaloosa County Library- Five books

Mark McCraw

Did You Come Home For Lunch?

Made with PosterMyWall.com

Feel free to review this book and others written by Mark McCraw on www.amazon.com.

www.ingramcontent.com/pod-product-compliance
Lightning Source LLC
Chambersburg PA
CBHW041144300726
48978CB00016B/1375